FEARSOME
CREATURES

Fearsome Creatures

by

Aliya Whiteley

BLACK SHUCK
SHADOWS

Black Shuck Books
www.BlackShuckBooks.co.uk

Versions of the following stories previously appeared as
follows:
'Day of the Dog' as an audio version by Drabblecast
(November 2018)
'Wrapped' in *Disturbing the Beast* (Boudicca Press, 2019)
'A Very Modern Monster' in *European Monsters* (Fox Spirit
Press, 2014)

First published in the UK by Black Shuck Books, 2020

978-1-913038-54-0

Day of the Dog

The afternoon the mayor plugged in the world's largest air-freshener I was in a bar with Petie, drinking orbitals. An orbital is a wheat beer with a dash of blackcurrant. It's a slow drink. It gives the world a sepia tint, like everything that's happening actually happened long ago, back in the good old days before everything got so complicated.

I was enjoying that sepia feeling, and Petie was talking about the time he found a slug in his bed, when the barman shushed him and turned up the volume on the television, which was on one of those metal arms that juts out from the wall, high up, next to the dusty bottles of champagne and tin plates that always seem to end up on the top shelves of bars. The screen showed the mayor, standing next to a plinth, and on it was one big red button, a bit like you might get on a tacky quiz show. The camera pulled back and showed the crowd.

'I think everyone in town is there except us,' I said, and the barman shushed us again.

'...the very first blanket coverage of air freshener to ever stretch across an entire town, making this a very proud moment for me, for you, and for every single one of us. A free, clean air for our free, clean town, making this a great place to raise your children, grow old, or simply sit outside and breathe in and out. And so, without further ado, I'm delighted to turn on the PuraGlade 3000, and I hope you all benefit from the freshness it will bring to our wonderful town.'

He pressed the giant red button and there was a moment of silence as everyone waited for their nostrils to report to their brains. Then there was an *aaaaaah!* And everyone sniffed and breathed and nodded and smiled at each other. It obviously smelled great.

The barman turned the volume back down.

'I guess this is the future then, Alice,' said Petie. 'Everyone smelling the same thing.'

'I wonder if it's pine,' I said. 'I hate pine.'

And then it wafted in through the open doorway, and we were breathing in lavender.

'Yay!' I said. 'I love lavender!' Admittedly, it was that synthetic lavender smell that got stuck in the back of your throat, but it was definitely better than pine.

'Now I can tell what my mother is smelling, right at this moment. I'm smelling it too. We're all smelling it.' Petie drained his orbital and banged down the glass. 'But what if I want to smell my own poo sometimes? What if I want to smell the rotted corpse of a cat that got run over? Shouldn't I be allowed to do that?'

'Nobody wants to do that,' said the barman. 'Another one?'

I shook my head.

'Oh, go on,' said Petie.

'I have to get going. I've got to change my library books today.'

'Oh, sure. You'd better hurry before they change all the books to the same one. Nobody should be reading anything different, should they?'

'It's just a smell,' I told him. I stood up and shook out my skirt, hoping he'd look at my legs. Instead he stared into his empty glass.

'I'm getting out of town before the stormtroopers arrive,' he said.

'That's the orbital talking. I'll call you later.'

He mumbled something. The barman and I exchanged glances, and then I left for the library. Outside, the sun was shining, and everyone was smiling for the first time since I can't remember when. Maybe ever. The lavender smell was less noticeable in the open. It just gave the air a little extra niceness. I caught a whiff of it every now and again as I walked down the street, and it made me feel pretty good. Lavender has healing properties; it gets used in herbal pillows and sleeping remedies. You can have a very relaxing bath in it. Bees like it, too. Although I couldn't say if they liked synthetic lavender much.

Outside the library, a dog was waiting for its master. It was on quite a short lead, tied to one of the railings, but it was in the shade, so I knew that wasn't the reason why it was crying. When a dog cries, it's different from a bark, or a howl. It's not even exactly a whimper. It's a soft, sad, unending sound. My dog made it all night after we got him neutered. He's dead now; he was my dog when I was a little girl. Every little girl should have a dog, I think. You'll never find a better friend.

I knelt down next to the dog and held out my hand so he could sniff me. Then I rubbed that sweet spot dogs have between their ears, but he kept on crying. He was a spaniel, a Cocker, with big brown patches and floppy ears. 'What is it, boy?' I asked.

His owner came out of the library. She was small and round and dressed in a woolly jumper that looked far too warm in the sunshine; her face was flushed, and she had that pulled-back expression that busy people get when they think time is slipping away from them. She came straight over to the dog and said, 'Oh, Teddy, I was only gone for a minute, honestly.'

'He really missed you,' I said, but the dog didn't wag his tail. He kept on crying. When she undid his lead and tugged at it, he wouldn't get up. He stayed sitting, head bowed.

'Come on, Teddy,' she said. She reached down to him, to pull him up by his collar I suppose, and he turned and bit her.

It was so weird. He didn't even growl first. He just turned and got her palm and bit down and held on, and she pulled back, and then there was this ripping sound and suddenly there was blood all over his mouth and her hand and she made this high-pitched squeal and fell over backwards, her arm against her chest. Teddy just licked his mouth with his long pink tongue. It was as if he'd been given a tasty treat.

People came running down the steps of the library, and they gathered around Teddy's owner, who was still squealing, and in the distance I thought I heard a dog barking, and then Teddy sat up and whined and I realised it was the sound of a lot of dogs barking. And it was getting louder.

Then the screaming started.

I didn't say anything to Teddy's owner, or to the crowd around her. To this day I still feel terrible about that, but when you're in a life or death situation, you either discover that you really really want to live and you're prepared to watch other people die in order to accomplish that, or you discover that you think life is not worth living if you're not still all being nice to each other. Having lived through that kind of situation I can tell you that I'm definitely in the first camp, and there's no point beating myself up about that. Instinct takes over. I ran as fast as

I have ever run, flat out, back to the bar, and I saw things on the way that still haunt me: bloodied things and slimy things and things that should have been parts of bodies and bodies that should have had hands and feet, and the dogs feeding, crunching down, working their way through the townspeople. I hit that bar at a hundred miles a second, and Petie and the barman were still there, watching the town square on the television, their mouths hanging open as the dogs ripped their way through what was left of the crowd.

They turned at the bang of the door, and I could see on their faces that they hadn't really grasped it, not yet, so I said, 'It's the air freshener. Gotta be the air freshener,' and closed the door behind me and dragged one of the long thin tables that usually sits up against the window in front of it. Yes, I know dogs can't turn door handles, but it seemed like a good idea at the time.

'The dogs are...' Petie said.

'Yeah.' I walked up to him, and took his face in my hands. Words spilled out of me, like a script; the things I once practised saying in the night, in the safety of a dark empty bedroom.

'I've always loved you. Right from Kindergarten. Even though you can be a moron sometimes. And I know that you're not good in an emergency – you couldn't even cope with a slug in your bed, for God's sake – so I already know that I'm going to have to take control of this situation to get us out of it alive, and that's fine. You don't owe me anything. You don't have to say you love me back. You just have to shut up and do what you're told, and I know that doesn't come easily to you, so please, try hard, okay?' I dropped my hands away from his stunned expression and looked at the barman. He returned my gaze without a qualm; I marked him down as useful. 'What's your name?'

'Marcus,' he said.

'Got any weapons around here?'

He smiled, crouched down behind the bar, and straightened up again with one hunting knife and one baseball bat. 'Will these do?'

'Nice,' I said.

'Never hurts to be prepared.'

'Right. Here's the plan. We need to get out of town. I happen to know that the woman who owns the hairdressers next door keeps her Range Rover parked out back. Now, the shop was shut, so she must have gone to the plugging in ceremony this morning, which means that she's dogmeat too by now, so let's hope she's left her keys in the car, and if not—'

'I can hotwire a car,' said Marcus.

'I'm liking you more and more,' I said.

'No, wait,' said Petie. 'Instead of leaving town, we should try to stop the smell, right? Then the dogs will go back to normal and people will be saved. We could drive the car into the big air freshener and smash it to pieces. We'd be heroes.'

'The only person I'm acting the hero for today is you, Petie,' I told him. 'That's a stupid plan, and we're not doing it. Firstly, the smell won't just dissipate because we've smashed up the freshener. Second, look at the TV. Are you seeing that?' There were more dogs arriving by the second, and some of them were carrying bits of people in their mouths while others just dove into the bodies with their snouts and ripped off gobbets of fat, or pulled out long meaty strands of intestine.

Behind us, there was a yipping sound. A terrier stood by the front door. I crouched down and eyeballed him through the legs of the long table. He scratched at the glass and whined, like a good boy waiting to be let in by his master.

'I'm not falling for that, mate,' I said.

The terrier sat down and waited. His tongue lolled out. He cocked his head to one side, as if he was thinking hard about something.

'Listen, it could work,' whispered Petie, close to my right ear. He had crouched down too, and he put one hand on my knee. For a moment I didn't smell lavender any more. I smelled him, that lovely innocent Petie smell. I took his hand from my knee, stood up, and chose the hunting knife. Marcus nodded, and took up the baseball bat. 'You're going to do this my way,' I said to Petie. 'No choice.'

'Who made you boss? You always got picked last for Dodgeball. When you announced you were going to run for class president everyone laughed until you sat down again.'

'This isn't school.'

'That's right!' he said, with a triumphant finger-point, as if he'd just won the argument. Then he looked out at the terrier, and I saw real fear cross his face. He was finally beginning to understand the situation. The little dog had been joined by a big one that I recognised – Mrs

Turner's Great Pyrenees, Holly. It had the sweetest temperament, and thick white fur that was so soft to the touch. I used to give it a stroke whenever I passed Mrs Turner on her porch; she loved to have a chat with whoever was walking by, and Holly adored being stroked. But now Holly's fur was matted with blood, and Mrs Turner was probably half-eaten on her porch, calling out through her terrible pain for help and wondering where the hell it all went wrong.

I pointed the knife at Petie. 'Get up. Get moving. We're going out through the back. Marcus, you take point.'

'Right,' said Marcus, and I followed his broad shoulders to the storeroom, with Petie grumbling all the way. Marcus threw his weight against the emergency exit bar and flung the door back; the daylight dazzled, and for a moment I couldn't see a thing. Then I made out the alley, with stacked orange crates of empty bottles, and the smell of lavender was swamped under the odour of stale beer. There were no dogs waiting for us. We only saw them when we got to the end of the alley, and there they were, sitting around the hairdresser's Range Rover as if they'd known the plan all along. I counted at least twenty, from a tiny Chihuahua to a gore-covered Great Dane who appeared to have half a baby stuck in its teeth.

'Crap,' I said.

'I'm going back,' announced Petie, and I gave him a small poke in the side with the hunting knife.

'They're staying by the car, though,' said Marcus. 'Why's that? They should be after us, but they're not.'

That's when it came to me. 'The smell! The beer smell. Come on.' I retreated back down the alley and selected from the nearest crate a bottle of Michelob with an inch of beer still sloshing around at the bottom. I poured it over Petie's head, then selected another for myself. Marcus got the idea too, and joined in.

'She's lost it,' said Petie, and I dragged him back to the entrance to the alley and frogmarched him to the Range Rover, all the time hoping I was right and pretending that I knew the stale beer trick was going to work.

It did. The dogs growled and backed off, even the Great Dane, and the car was unlocked, and I threw Petie on to the back seat and took the front passenger seat while Marcus got behind the wheel and fiddled around under the dashboard. The engine started, an educated purr that suited such an expensive car, and I have to admit I really enjoyed the sensation of being ferried around town in that huge, wonderful wagon, hearing the occasional dog go splat under the wheels.

We made it to the edge of town, and up ahead was a road blockade, with tanks and soldiers and a few townspeople I recognised, hanging around, crying and nursing flesh wounds.

Marcus pulled over and stopped the car. I turned round to Petie. 'It's okay,' I said. 'It's going to be okay now.'

'Yeah,' he said. He stared at his hands, in his lap. 'Thanks.'

And I knew, in that moment, that in all the possible futures that lay before us, there wasn't one in which Petie and I would get married, and have kids, and live a wonderful life together. He would never forget the things I'd done that day. He'd never get over the fact that I saved him.

~

Forty-Eight Years Later

'Are you ready?' I said.

Marcus nodded. I stroked his cheek through the balaclava. Even after all these years, he still looked darned fine in his action gear. He worked out five times a week and attended a local Dojo at the weekend. And I did my bit, too; being seventy really wasn't so bad, as long we both kept moving and popped the prescribed pills. Sometimes, I have to admit, I wondered what we kept moving for, particularly after the kids left home and the government work dried up. I mean, we could have opted for a couples euth programme and our pensions would have covered it – no back-street doctor skimping on the morphine for us – but we felt there was still something lying up ahead for us. And we were so right.

'Now.'

I smeared the putty around the window frame, then gave the glass a soft tap; it came free, and Marcus caught it, and laid it down on the well-kept lawn, where it reflected the glint of the full moon. We repeated the process with the inner pane, and then it was just a matter of climbing inside, disabling the alarm system, and locating our target.

We found him sleeping in the basement, propped on a stool in front of his very own private mahogany bar, an empty martini glass in front of him, with a little pink paper umbrella leaning against the lip. From my viewpoint on the stairs, looking at his slim back and curly brown hair, he looked the same as ever. It was only when I spoke and he swivelled to face me that I realised time had caught up with him too. In fact, it had chased him down and savaged him, scoring his face with deep lines that ran from his eyes to his sagging chin.

'Petie,' I said. 'You should have known better. Got any wheat beer?'

Marcus touched my shoulder, and we moved into the room, to join Petie at the bar. Once behind it, Marcus looked comfortable, pulling off his balaclava and searching through the cupboards. 'Got the beer. And some blackcurrant cordial.'

'Perfect. Make me an orbital, will you? And one for our host.' I hadn't had one since that day when the dogs turned bad; I wondered if it was going to be as fantastic as I remembered. It had been heaven, with the sunshine coming through the windows and the local news channel playing on the portable television above the row of optics, running some piece about a new sculpture commissioned for the town hall, or a change to the train timetable.

'What are you doing here, Alice?' said Petie, as his orbital was placed in front of him. Funnily enough, he didn't look that surprised to see me. There was a settled air of resignation in the way his shoulders slumped.

'You thought you could start it up, all over again, and we wouldn't find out?'

'It's totally different this time around. It's got nothing to do with you.'

'Petie, Petie, Petie,' I said, and I realised how hard the years had made me, that I could speak to him, my lost first love, in that tone of voice. I hated myself as I told him, 'After you walked away from me that day, Marcus and I started stamping out the global market in mass smells for a living. Of course, we had to let some other people die, or get actively involved in making them dead, in order to save the important ones, but that's life all over, isn't it?'

'Is it?' said Petie.

'You don't agree?' I sipped my orbital. It was not as I remembered it, to be honest. Maybe wheat beer had changed over the past forty years. 'I don't understand you, to be honest. You opted out. You didn't want to save anyone. So why have you suddenly decided to start killing them? They're two sides of the same coin. If you don't like one, you won't enjoy the other.'

'Nobody's going to die!'

'They will when you plug in that giant air freshener tomorrow morning. How did you talk the townsfolk into it? Are memories so short, nowadays? How did you get elected Mayor, anyway? Surely running a town requires a backbone?'

He stood up, his knees wobbling; he was already so drunk he could hardly stand. 'It's not an air freshener,' he said, with a burst of venomous energy, 'It's a deodoriser.'

'A what?'

'It removes all smells. Do you understand? All smells. No more plug-in pine-fresh scents. No more all trying to smell the same thing. We are all going to smell nothing but real, true smells. This town will be united in our clean, unbothered nostrils.'

'What about the dogs?'

'What about them? It's got nothing to do with the dogs, don't you get it? There won't be any smell to upset the dogs. This is not about the fucking dogs.' His legs gave out, and he slumped to the floor. 'It's about you and me. You and me, and what you took away from me.'

'You and me? There's more important stuff out there than you and me. You don't know what will happen when you turn that giant deodoriser on. You have no idea.'

'That's right!' He dropped his head to his chest. For a moment I thought he was asleep, but then I heard quiet, soft sobbing, and there was a pain in my heart, the kind I hadn't felt for years. I looked up at Marcus, and he nodded. Good old Marcus, my dependable hero of a husband, knowing me better than I knew myself. With his approval, I felt no problem with kneeling down beside Petie, stroking his hair, whispering to him of the things I had been thinking all these years.

'Listen, remember that slug in your bed? The one that got there, somehow, magically, and you never knew how?'

He straightened up. 'You put it there!'

'No, you complete moron. That's just my point. Nobody put it there. There's no big reason for everything. You're looking at the details of your life and trying to make sense of them, right? Trying to understand that day, so many years ago, when the dogs turned on us all and I got you out of town. But that day was like a slug in your bed. It didn't mean anything. And you can't make it mean something, no matter what you do. You'll always be that guy who survived. And being a survivor is just the same as being dead with a longer sell-by-date on the top of your packet. That's all.'

'That's not true!' he shouted. 'You ruined me! I could have saved everyone! We could have made it to the town square, and destroyed that freshener, and those people would still be alive!'

'It was too late.'

'It wasn't.' He took a deep breath, and smiled at me. I saw the boy once again, in that smile. 'It really wasn't.'

'In that case, I'm sorry. I'm sorry I stopped you from saving everyone. But now you have a chance to be a real hero. You can get a whole new set of people out of danger. Give up on the deodoriser. You plug that thing in, and who knows what will happen? Let's not find out, okay?' I helped him up, and we sat back on the stools, side by side, with Marcus behind the bar pretending to mind his own business, just like old times.

'Thanks,' Petie said. He sighed. 'What happens if I say no?'

I glanced at Marcus. 'Something not nice.'

'Wow. Really? You'd let your friend here do something not nice to me?'

'He's not my friend. He's my husband. And I'd do it myself.'

He took a big gulp of his orbital. I followed suit. 'I always did wonder about that slug. I guess I'll never know, now.'

'So what's your answer?'

'Should I be a hero your way or my way, do you mean? I think it won't mean anything if I don't do it my way.'

'Right,' I said. 'Have it your way.'

And he did.

Marcus helped me clean up afterwards. We made it look like suicide, and got rid of the remains of the orbitals, and put the glass panes back in the window frames as we left the way we had entered. Then we went down to the town square and sabotaged that enormous deodoriser, so it would never be turned on. One more attempt to make us all the same, stamped out. I truly believe we shouldn't all have to smell the same things, because we're not all the same type of person. Some of us are heroes.

We've saved many people, over the years, Marcus and I. I think my favourite was Petie, though. My first, and my favourite.

The Lovers That Lie Down in Fields

Walk me home, she'd said, during the waltz.

He stood outside the main door as the men sauntered past, and then the girls emerged in their twos and threes, bunched and giggling. They threw looks his way. Will waited: tall, awkward, blushing.

When Sarah emerged, she seemed not to know that he was there. Her chin was tucked in as she fiddled with the ivory buttons on her green coat. It took an age. Then she looked up and smiled as if to say *there you are: nothing else matters.*

It was a fine night.

He had maybe three miles until they reached her father's house, but in that time she could be his. They left the hall behind them and headed out of the village, past the church and the graveyard, past the school building where he had sat behind her every day, watching her make her letters so carefully. Then they were out into the country, and the fields of the estate fell away from the long ridge, alive with wheat. The weather had held throughout August and the stalks were long in the light of the three-quarter moon.

Neither of them spoke.

He would start threshing next week, under the instruction of Imogen's father, who had been taken on at the big house as foreman. The days would be hard, the air scratchy with chaff, but he did not need to think of it now, in the coolness of her presence. She was as fresh as grass in her coat.

He wanted to touch her. He put his hand down casually, and slid his finger along the fold of her dress. It was slippery, not soft at all, but stiff. The dress encased her. The Phoebe he wanted to know was underneath it, slim and breathing.

'Good dance, weren't it?' he said, just to have her speak. His own voice was a tragedy of his commonness, but he had to talk.

'Yes,' she said. 'I enjoyed it.'

She was well-spoken, training to be a secretary. She took the bus every day to town, to study at the municipal college. She knew more than him on nearly every subject, but Will knew the soil , its growths and creations. She could never touch that knowledge; he did not want her to.

'You'll be working with father next week,' she said. How forced she sounded.

'Starting at top field, aye.'

She looked out over the fields, her head turned away from him, so he was free to take in the line of her neck, the pinching of the material where her shoulder blade joined her back. 'It'll all be bare, after that. Moving to winter.'

'Christmas,' he said. He knew she liked Christmas, had seen her at church dressed in red, her eyes alive with the cold before they all went in for service, and the bells ringing loud. She had seemed happy and free to him, separate from everyone who surrounded her, even her family.

But she turned to him, and said with passion, 'Oh, no talk of Christmas yet!'

He could not think of things to say to her that she would like; she did not care for his conversation. They had been better dancing, without this need to speak, to fill silence.

'I liked the waltz,' she said, shyly, as if she had read his thoughts. Holding her, obeying the music and guiding her within it.

'Me too,' he said.

She took his hand, squeezed it. Her grip was intense and cold, and it surprised him utterly, but then she pulled away and left him, standing there; she slid away like water spilling, and she ran, ran into the wheat, away from him. He could not move, he did not know what to make of it, except for the pain of the separation. She had rejected him, she needed to escape, but then she called, 'Come on!' over her shoulder. He leapt down, and plunged into the wheat after her, watching her run away, he would never catch her, but slowly, slowly, yes, he was coming to her and she could not outrun him, not forever.

He drew level. Her breathing was loud as he passed her, then turned to her as she ran into him. The force of her was strong but he held her, with her long red hair worked loose of its knots and the top button of the neck of her coat undone; he felt certain she would simply rise up out of the constraints of her clothes and be gone, and even that he could follow. He could rise too, they would float above the land, turn into one fine being of light and air.

Instead they fell. She pulled him down. The wheat flattened beneath them, and he was on top of her, surely she couldn't bear his weight, and he put down his hands on either side of her shoulders to lift himself.

She kissed him.

Such a small, clean mouth on his.

It was not comfortable; the stalks stuck into his hands and knees, and he could not seem to fit his mouth to hers properly, but oh, it was good. To want, and be wanted. To have this proof, undeniable, that she felt for him and his dreams did not have to live only in his head, in the moments between exhaustion and sleep at the end of the working day. It was not as he had hoped it would be, and it was everything.

She broke the kiss and he dropped his head to her chest, pressing his ear to the strange curve. Her coat had ridden up and wrinkled.

'I can't bear to go back,' said Phoebe.

The wheat was moving around them. The sound of the wind came from very far away. It was the sound of the world to which they had to return. Not yet, not yet.

'I don't know how to stay here,' she said.

'We could get married.' There, he had said it. The completion of his dream. The words were their own church, better than the one in the village. Just to speak it, to have her listen, was sacred.

'It's not marriage that I'm talking about, Will. It's – I don't know. It's this.' Her eyes were on the stalks that sprang upright around them.

'The field?'

'It goes on forever,' she said. 'In the moonlight.'

It didn't. It went as far as the boundary with Chaddick's land, and then there was the county border. He could not understand her, even though he was so close, on her. And she had dismissed his proposal in a way that hurt him deeply. His special words had been waved away as if she could never take it seriously. It was taking time for the extent of the wound to sink in, but it was getting deeper, deeper. He felt tears come to his eyes and made no attempt to stop them, nor turn his face away. He let them drip down his face and on to hers. He wanted her to feel them.

'No no no,' she said. She took his animal face in her hands.

'Why don't you want me?' he asked her, humbly, and she said, 'I do want you, Will. I want you and me together. But not in a church, can't you understand? Not in a starched suit that makes you stand funny, and me in a white dress chosen from the shop in town. I want us to stay like this. Nothing but this. Can we do that?'

She kissed him again, long, and his body began its reply to her question – yes, they could be this, this place, within this light. He shivered and felt her mouth open underneath his; her small tongue was in his mouth. He lowered his weight and let the length of him come up against her, then he moved with intent, so she could feel him properly. She wriggled, her coat bunched. It was too much, he was so close to being inside her, he could be—

Nothing but this, forever.

The wind stopped moving through the wheat.

The stalks surged towards them, straining at the soil, and wrapped themselves around his arms, their legs, their joined thighs.

The sharp ears pierced their skin, found their

blood, and drank. The field sucked at them with the blind neediness of a baby. It was slowly satisfied, fed, filled.

When the blood was taken, Will and Phoebe watched the stalks rip free, leaving dry holes in their emptied bodies. They stayed so still as the ground grumbled, then parted, splitting into long cracks that swallowed their skin and bones and took them down deep.

What then?

Then time started again, and this time it ran. It was fast and sleek, it sped over seasons, and the changing world meant nothing to the well-fed field.

Let them thresh the wheat, and let the wheat regrow. There is blood in the soil, and love sealed tight. The land sucks what it needs, and takes the rest for meat.

One night, to the hum of the cars on the motorway, the ground disgorges a coat that was once green, spitting forth a remain of grey rags. The stalks of wheat sway towards the turning wheels on the road, waiting for the lovers that will stop their journeys to lie down and be taken, that will find a way to forever.

Luisa Opines

He first came to my door when my aunt was not at home. He had a smile prepared. It was a good one, with teeth.

'I'm asking questions,' he said. 'It's for a survey.' He pointed to a badge on his shirt. It was purple, with white writing on it, and below that was a picture of him, wearing the same smile. It read:

PEEL

'My aunt will be back later,' I said. 'I can tell her you called round.'

'Actually,' he said, 'I can ask you. If that's okay? Just a question, but the results are used to make improvements, inform decisions, that sort of thing.'

I was flattered, in the way that only the young can be when given sudden attention by a stranger. But I did not invite him in. I was not that stupid. 'Ask away,' I said, crossing my arms over my chest.

He produced a small rectangular device from the black bag. The flat surface glowed. 'My tablet,' he said. 'It's all technology nowadays.'

'What does it do?'

'Haven't you seen one before?' He seemed surprised, but held the tablet out so I could see it clearly. 'I can record your answers by touching the screen. See?' He demonstrated, his fingers fast and agile, his long nails tapping. I craned my head to see; it was an intriguing invention. I liked the strange light it created. 'Right. Here goes. What do you think the crime rate is in your neighborhood?'

'I don't think there is any crime around here, is there?' I said. We lived in the deep dark wood, my aunt and I, with nobody nearby for miles and miles. I'd never felt unsafe, even for a moment. Boredom was my usual emotion. Grinding, desperate boredom for my safe little life.

'Nothing at all?' He frowned, and tapped the screen.

'Unless you count the animals,' I joked. 'They're up to all sorts, I bet.'

He laughed. 'Of course,' he said. 'Plenty of murder and mayhem there. Right. Can I ask you – if the crime level went up, would you think about relocating to a different neighbourhood?'

I pretended that the cottage and the garden and the decisions belonged to me. It came quite easily; I was at that age. 'Yes, I think I would.'

He nodded. 'Wise,' he said. 'And what if the crime level dropped? Would you feel safer then?'

'Well, it can't drop. I'm perfectly safe.'

'Yes,' he said. 'Sorry. Stupid question.' He swiped the screen, and smiled again. 'Right, that's it. Thank you for your time.'

'You're welcome.' I couldn't see that I'd been any help to him, and that bothered me. I wanted to produce the kind of answers that informed all the big decisions that his people were making, but I didn't know anything and hadn't been anywhere. All I knew was the cottage, and the little garden out the back for growing vegetables. Only an old encyclopedia, kept on the high shelf in the parlour, gave me any idea of what the world was really like. I wasn't even allowed to go out gathering berries and mushrooms with my aunt. And now the most exciting thing that had ever happened to me was about to end.

'One last thing,' he said.

'Yes?' Oh, I was so eager. My heart breaks for the girl I was.

'Can I come back next week with a few more questions? There are new surveys popping up all the time, you see. '

'You must be busy.'

'I like it,' he said. 'Is that okay?'

'Yes, that's fine, although I don't know much about anything, I'm afraid.'

'Oh, you'll be perfect. You were a big help today. Can I take your name for the records?'

'Luisa,' I said. 'Can I ask *you* a question?'

'Hah! You're getting in the swing of this. Yes, of course. Ask away.'

'Is that your name? Peel?'

'That's right.' He pointed to his badge again, and stepped a little closer so I could read the smaller writing at the bottom.

FOREST INFORMATICA

'See?' he said, and I did. I saw his picture and his face, and the smile on both, and I liked them.

~

Peel asked me so many questions over the months that followed, always arriving a few minutes after the departure of my aunt. She would put on her cloak and head out into the forest, and I would wait in a state of high excitement for the knock at the door which would always follow. He had immaculate timing.

'You're in a good mood,' my aunt would often say, when she returned home to find me humming as I washed the floor, or did one of the many tasks she concocted to fill my days.

'I am,' I always agreed. 'I really am.'

She was happier too, I think, because I'd stopped asking her so many questions of my own, such as where my parents were and whether I could go with her when she left the cottage. I had a fresh purpose. I answered questions.

'On a scale of one to five, how do you feel about holidaying in hot countries?'

I really wasn't a fan of them, even though I'd

never been anywhere, so that turned out to be a one.

'If you were to open a savings account, what rate of interest would you be looking for?'

Once he'd explained the concepts of both savings accounts and interest to me I opted for at least two per cent.

'Indicating your choice on the screen, what shade of green do you find most attractive in a frozen pea?'

I particularly liked the questions for which he held out the tablet towards me. I touched the screen, with authority, no matter what I knew or didn't know. The nonsensical nature of the things he asked me were no barrier to my belief that I had become important. I imagined he belonged to a place where they cherished my responses, and I even allowed myself to believe that if I gave enough answers that pleased him, he'd ask me to go back there with him.

'What qualities do you look for in a soft drink? Touch all the words that apply.'

I opted for tasty, refreshing, sparkling, and non-fattening.

His shoes were always grey suede, and he wore trousers and a shirt that were as black as his swept-back hair. He was both young and old to me; I felt he understood me as an equal, but he could have commanded me and I would have obeyed. Perhaps it's easier to say he was my everything. I wanted so desperately to impress him but how could I do that when nothing had happened to me? I wished for an event to come along to make me more interesting.

And then an event happened.

My aunt did not come home.

~

I sat at the table and picked at my fingernails until the sun had set. Then I opened the door and stared out at the night. The dark trees seemed closer, thicker. Their leaves hissed in the wind with ominous intent.

The first question Peel had ever asked me came into my mind, along with my blithe reply. *There is no crime*, I had told him. Was that true? What did I know about it? Just because fear and pain had not burst through my door, it did not mean that it was not waiting for me to come to it.

Something huffed, out in the night. Something took a breath.

I slammed the door and ran to my bed. I pulled the covers over my head, and lay there, shivering, for hours. I would not sleep, it was an impossibility; I would never sleep again, I could never sleep ag—

Knock knock

My eyes opened to the bright light of late morning.

For a moment I was peaceful, wondering why my aunt had not woken me to start my many duties. Then my heart crashed at the memory of the night before, and I sprang up to run to the door, thinking she must be home, she had lost her key, she had been hurt but she was back, and I threw open the door to find Peel standing there, holding his tablet out with the screen facing me. Upon it were written two words, in thick black letters:

**DEEPEST
SYMPATHIES**

'We're so sorry,' he said.

'What?'

'Your aunt. We're so sorry she's missing.'

'But I—'

'Word travels fast in the forest. We're all thinking of you.' I'd never seen him without a smile before. Instead he wore an expression of intense sympathy, giving him wrinkles around his forehead and mouth, and between his eyes. It made his skin look loose, pouchy.

'Can you help me find her?' I said.

'Of course. I'll put out the word right now.' He turned around the tablet and began to tap on it.

'I meant – can you come with me, if I go and look for her? Please?'

'Trust me,' he said. 'This will help.'

I watched him at work, his fingers fast, his expression so serious. All I wanted was for him to take over, to say *quick, pack some food and water, grab supplies, lock up the cottage, I know a place where she might be, this way, follow me* but he didn't.

'I should go,' I told him, told myself.

You're in a good mood, she had said to me, many times, and I had agreed. She had felt happy because I was happy.

'Really?' said Peel.

'I have to try to find her. I owe it to her.'

'Wait,' he said. 'Before you set off, can I ask you a quick question?'

'I'm not really—'

He turned the tablet back to face me once more. 'Could you indicate on the screen what expression best represents your current emotional state?'

Four little cartoon faces: Happy face, sad face, surprised face, angry face. I reached out and touched the sad face. It was blue, with two tears rolling from the downturned eyes.

'Thanks,' he said. 'Right. Well. I'll leave you to it in this difficult time. Thoughts and prayers.'

'I'll find her, though,' I said, but all I could think of was how useless I was, and how little I knew of that great big forest out there: the one that Peel knew, and moved through.

'Well, good luck,' he said.

He really wasn't going to offer to come with me.

~

Where to go when there are no trails, no clues?

I did not travel in any direction that could be found on a compass, so much as try to move towards hope. I could not say if it took me in a straight line or round in circles. The path outside the door soon petered away to nothing so I abandoned the pretence of following anything. The cottage was swallowed up by the trees behind me, and the dim rays of light that managed to break through the thick leaves overhead gave me no indication of where the sun sat in the sky. There were only the dense greens and browns of plants and earth. I saw no animals at all, and for that I was grateful. But I imagined their eyes upon me.

I forced myself to call out as I walked, and the forest swallowed the sound.

'Aunt? Auntie?'

Eventually my throat grew sore. I stopped calling out, and searched her out only with my eyes. I stumbled down a grassy hillock and found older, thicker trees with wet ferns clustered around their trunks, and thick patches of mushrooms growing in abundance between them. Could this be the very place my aunt visited every week to collect our supplies?

'Aunt!' I croaked.

It was no good. Not a trace of a footprint, not one broken frond, to show she might have passed this way. I collected some mushrooms and put them in the basket I carried. It was getting dark quickly; the day was coming to an end. *Be brave*, I told myself. *I must be brave.*

The biggest tree had split in its middle, creating a small hollow, just big enough to crawl inside. It was not much, but it offered more protection than simply lying on the ground. I got down on my hands and knees and crawled through the slimy mushrooms to slip inside, on the damp earth, as the last of the daylight ebbed away. There was only my breathing in the cold air, and the hard ground, and the webs of the spiders against my face, and the creaking of the wood. But soon it seemed that the sounds were becoming rhythmic and soothing, and the ground and air were growing warmer, softer, and I slept.

'Knock knock.'

What is it about the illusion of waking peacefully, as if one is still in a warm, safe bed, only to have the real world come crashing down? The soreness of my body was sudden and agonising; I was balled up tight in the tree, covered in slime trails, with a snail on my cheek. I picked it off and struggled out of the hollow.

Peel stood there, amidst the ferns, looking clean and handsome, his white teeth gleaming. 'Hello,' he said. 'How would you feel about answering a question?'

'Not half as good as I'd feel about a hot bath and some breakfast,' I told him. 'How did you find me?'

'No sign of your aunt,' he said. 'That's sad, isn't it? Sad.' He made his sad face, and the skin of his cheeks and forehead sagged. 'Will you be going on, or turning back?'

'I don't think I know which way is back.' I picked some mushrooms, and ate them with some of the bread I'd packed in my basket. It was a chillier morning.

'Onwards it is, then.'

'Was that the question?'

'Ha! Of course not!' He produced his tablet and turned the screen to me. How bright and soothing it was in the dim light of the forest. 'Right. Which of these qualities do you most value in a hand soap? Choose all that apply.'

- A floral scent
- Antibacterial properties
- Creamy lather
- Long-lasting bar
- Value for money
- Natural ingredients
- Ethical packaging

'What's ethical packaging?' I asked.

'Can you trust it?' he said, after some consideration.

'Can I trust the bar of soap?' It wasn't a quality I'd thought about in regards to soap, but I selected it, along with the creamy lather and natural ingredients. Three seemed like a good number of things to choose.

'Thank you so much,' Peel said. 'Have a great day!'

'Wait – did you hear anything? About where my aunt could be?'

'I'll check...' he said. He tapped the screen. 'Not yet. But I will. Have a little faith.'

'Fine,' I said. I picked up my basket and started walking. When I looked back over my shoulder, Peel was nowhere to be seen.

~

The second day of searching was both worse and better than the first. My illusions were at an end; I would not find her. And wasn't she the woman who had kept me tied to chores, refused to tell me my history, failed to prepare me for the world? Perhaps she had decided to leave, and never return. Was she capable of such an act?

I finally began to understand that I did not really know her at all.

You're in a good mood – she had said. And then she had been in a good mood too. I hung on to that thought above all others.

Onwards, onwards. I came across a dappled clearing with a cheery stream, and I washed, and drank my fill of good clean water. The trees shrank back beyond, and I emerged into a field of tall wild flowers of blue; I ran through it with abandon, my basket swinging, to plunge into the dense trees once more. Part of me despaired even while I began to see the forest through fresh eyes. It was not a place of fear and cruelty. It had beauty within it.

Then I came across the body.

The blood, smeared over the trunk, had a strong smell unlike anything I had come across before. I stopped walking and stared at the mess. It was a body, yes, a body in pieces, ripped apart. An arm, separated from a shoulder, and legs broken and splayed. Panic overtook me. *Auntie*, I thought, and fell to my knees, but then I saw the hooves and the fat under the pink flesh, and I realised it was not human, but pig. A pig had been killed here, dismembered with great force, by something large. Something powerful.

I got to my feet. I took small, slow steps backwards, and retreated until I could not smell the blood anymore.

And so onwards in a different direction, until the light began to fade.

It was going to be a much colder night. Already I could feel the icy fingers of the night on my skin. But there, up ahead, like an answer to a prayer, was a rocky outcropping with a gap between two boulders, just wide enough to admit me. I clambered up and lowered myself in to find a small cave with a mossy floor – and even a blanket, waiting for me. How could that be? I refused to worry myself about the blanket until the morning. I pulled it around myself in the darkness, and slept the sleep of one who has walked too far and seen too much. I didn't know it then, but I was growing up.

'Knock knock.'

I knew who it was before I opened my eyes. When I climbed from the cave, with blanket and basket, there he was, looking as handsome as ever.

'Good morning,' he said. 'I have great news!

The question of where your aunt might be was raised as a survey yesterday, and eighty-four per cent of people didn't know. Five per cent claimed she was dead, and eleven per cent claimed that her disappearance was a hoax.'

I barely listened. The morning light had revealed the blanket was not a blanket at all. It was my aunt's cloak. I held it out, half-expecting her to walk up and take it. But there was only Peel, smiling at me.

'What's that?' he said.

'It's hers. Her cloak.'

'No,' he said, 'Really? Hang on, I'll tell everyone.' He took out his tablet and tapped on it.

'She must have slept here,' I said. 'Why would she leave her cloak behind? I don't understand.'

'I'll ask around, see if anyone knows.'

'That's not going to help,' I told him. 'And I should get going. She can't be far away.'

'Before you set off, could you tell me what you think of this statement? *A nearly professional standard of home decorating can be achieved by a DIY approach if the right materials are used.* Strongly agree, agree, neutral, disagree, strongly disagree?'

'No more questions.'

He held the tablet up to my face, 'Easier to answer it than to opt out,' he said. 'It takes an age to opt out. Lots of forms to fill in.'

'I'm not – fine, then.' I touched the screen, randomly, not caring where my finger landed, and he stepped back.

'Thanks,' he said. 'More walking today?'

'Yes,' I said, shortly. I shook out my aunt's cloak and put it on. It was warm, red wool with a silk lining, and I was grateful for it in the cold morning air. But I couldn't help but think of her without it. Freezing. Hungry. Desperate.

Or maybe not. Maybe she was already back home, now, and I was the one who was lost.

'Good luck!' called Peel, as I stomped away.

~

Where did I come from?

I thought about that question as I forced my sore legs to take me onwards.

I had come from a small cottage. It was so far behind me, the path to return unclear. I might never return.

In another sense, the place where I had come from was invisible to me. I had no idea who my parents were, and if I did not find my aunt, I would never know.

When I find you... I vowed. The words sounded in my mind, in time with my footsteps. *When I find you, I'll make you tell me. I'll make you take me home.*

Wrapped in her cloak, I felt closer to her than ever before. Surely she was close. Surely I would get my answers.

On through the forest, everything familiar and yet strange, no way to tell where I would end up. How big can a forest be? What lies beyond it?

~

A cottage.

A perfect little cottage, situated in a clearing, stumbled upon as if by accident, as if by design.

It was not my cottage, but it was very like it. It had the same oak door and neat square windows. But it was too clean and new. It looked unlived in. And it was, perhaps, a little too square on the windows, and when I knocked the sound of my fist on the wood was hollow.

'Come in!' called a voice I knew.

I turned the handle and went inside, into a parlour so very like, through a kitchen nearly the same, to a room almost identical to my aunt's bedroom.

There she lay, tucked up in bed, smiling.

'It's so lovely to see you, Luisa, dear,' she said. 'I hope you're in a good mood. You know I love it when you're in a good mood.'

'Stop it,' I said.

The smile dropped from her face. The skin around her mouth and eyes was loose, pouchy. 'I don't know what you mean,' she said.

'Come out of there right now.'

'But it's me! Your aunt!'

'Do you think I'm an idiot?' I said. 'You killed her.'

'I did no such thing! I eat pigs, not humans. Besides, we're friends, aren't we? Friends don't eat each other's relatives.'

'Are we, Peel?' I asked. 'Are we really friends? Come on, get out of that disguise.'

'Fine,' said Peel. He put his hands to my aunt's hair and pulled, and the skin rolled away in one piece. But the handsome young man I was expecting to see was not underneath. Instead I found myself face to face with a great grey wolf, still tucked up in bed: its mouth fixed in a permanent grin, its teeth long and white, and its black eyes filled with sharp intent. 'Well,' it said. 'Now we can see each other properly. Are you scared?'

'No,' I said.

'On a scale of one to five, where would you place your fear right now?'

'If you didn't kill my aunt,' I said, 'why do you have her skin?'

'I made it. I created it from the answers to the questions I ask. She loved to answer questions too, you see. She would await my knock at the door, on the moment after you fell asleep, every night. We used to have a fine old time together.' He held up one huge hairy paw. 'And I swear I don't know where she went. She never breathed a word about leaving to me. It doesn't matter, anyway. I have her thoughts and feelings, her likes and dislikes, right here.' He held up the discarded skin: an aunt-shaped costume for a wolf to wear. It rustled, a little, and let out a small whine.

'She really did leave me,' I said. 'I don't understand it. I thought she loved me.'

'Perhaps you never asked her the right questions,' suggested Peel. He threw back the bedsheets and stood up. How tall he was; his ears nearly touched the ceiling. He scooped up the skin and crossed the room on his wolf paws, and I shrank back as he passed by me to open the wardrobe, revealing a strong white light inside. 'Come on,' he said. 'Come right this way while I hang her up.'

He stepped into the wardrobe and I followed, and we were both in a long corridor, stretching far into the distance, lit very brightly by no light source I could see. Two long silver poles, running horizontally on either side of us, gleamed like the screen of his tablet, and skins, many skins, hung from the poles on hangers. The corridor could not possibly have been inside the cottage; I felt that it wasn't in the forest either, but was part of some other world where everything was sharp and cold and very flat.

We walked, side by side, into that world, until he said, 'Here we are.' He stopped beside an empty hanger, and put my aunt's skin back upon it. Then he took down the one next to it, and I saw it was me. I recognised myself straight away. Peel climbed inside, and in a blur the illusion of my skin became a reality. He was me.

'I'm really not a fan of holidaying in hot countries,' he said. 'And hand soap has to have a creamy lather.'

He was a thief. And it seemed to me, at that moment, that his thievery was worse than any other crime he could have committed. I would have preferred that he murdered me.

'Why?' I whispered. 'Why?'

We walked onwards, down the long corridor, until we came to a metal door with no handle. 'In here,' he said.

~

I've been here in this world ever since, the world of wolves in costumes made of questions. They wander around in the brightness, asking each other questions, telling little jokes, sometimes shouting out strange statements, pretending to be human. Sometimes they band together, all the ones who share a certain opinion about hand soap or foreign holidays, and swagger around arm in arm.

I'm lost amongst them.

Occasionally I see myself in the crowd, and I call out, 'Help!', but my skin turns and plunges back into the crowd. I think maybe Peel doesn't recognise me. Perhaps I don't look like myself anymore.

I don't know who I am, just as I didn't know Peel, and I didn't know my aunt. But here, here in the wolf world, it doesn't matter. Everyone has their straightforward answers ready to so many questions that can be thought about without the fear or pain that I found in the forest. It's easier to be certain about things here.

I've been asking myself: on a scale of one to ten, how much would I like to return to the life I had before, in the cottage, trying to understand anyone, including myself?

Does it matter where I came from if I'm not going anywhere?

I'm not certain. Put me down as a maybe.

Wrapped

— Part One —

No great evil has befallen any of us yet. I suppose it is only a matter of time until an accident lays low one of the workers, or my skirts tangle in a rope and trip me up, or a sandstorm descends. Then Khefatra will receive the blame.

Khefatra. Her mask is a frightening sight to behold. The first guides panicked and ran from the burial chamber when we opened the outer sarcophagus, but even back in the relative safety of my tent I can understand how our workers believe she holds a curse; to simply look upon the bronze head that bears her carved visage is to feel queasy. Is it an accurate depiction of her, or does it represent the feelings of those who served her? That open, contorted mouth, and the thick wrinkles around the eyes and nose, are unlike anything I have seen. The masks of the dead are meant to be serene in their countenance; this is a figure disturbed, and disturbing.

I wish I could have known her.

I have spent my life in pursuit of her, and I maintain my theory that she was a ruler of her people. A forgotten Pharaoh, the first clue to her importance to be found in the fact that her name had been scratched through in so many records: what did she do to deserve such a fate? Only painstaking research, the piecing together of clues that others have attempted to destroy, led me to suspect that her burial chamber remained intact, to be found under the sand in an area that fell back under the control of the ancient Libyans shortly after her death. And so my dear Nigel arranged funding and permissions, and here we are, at the culmination of my great undertaking.

Culmination? Hardly. As I write I realise that the word is inappropriate. Yes, I have found her chamber. I have already documented what has been found within: the ushabti containing the dust that is all that now remains of her vital organs; the small clay boats with linen sails that lasted no more than an hour in the desert air before disintegrating. But this is only the beginning of my work. Now I must hunt, and translate, and find irrefutable evidence of her reign, and of what befell her. This will finally satisfy my curiosity, and also secure my place amongst the works of those who have long inspired me: Carter, Maspero, and my own father.

Tonight, as my dependable Waleed pulled me back up from the chamber, hefting upon the rope attached to the canvas sling which has become my vehicle to Khefatra's remains, I found Nigel waiting for me by the mouth of the hole to offer me tea. I told him he was a marvel, and he replied with a warm smile that I, in fact, was the marvellous one. His admiration for my skills as an archaeologist and researcher has long been one of the greatest blessings of my life. I remember when he first proposed, at Kew, under a potted palm, and he said I was a true original. I asked him, then, if he felt he could support me in my endeavours rather than seek to control or curtail them.

"Ursula Templeton," he said to me then, in words that will stay with me forever, "you are unique. Your work is as important to me as it is to you. It must continue. I will make certain that it does."

I chose my husband wisely. Even if he does snore, rather: a sound that is currently assailing me as I write, sitting across the tent from the bed at the small travelling desk that accompanies me on all of my travels.

Snoring is a small price to pay for a man who understands me so. I never thought to find one. I am out of my time, and therefore must select allies carefully who will make sure I am not imprisoned in the strictures that society sets upon us.

We are a pair, Nigel and I. I provide the knowledge and the money (one must remain forever grateful for father's work and the inheritance it provided) and Nigel greases the wheels of the world with his charm. How could the Libyan government refuse his requests? I know I could not.

~

15th April

At the end of this long and terrible day I wish to write only one word.

Enough.

But this journal is for posterity, not for my own whim. So I must record the fact that Khefatra is no longer mine alone. She is to be taken from me under the guise of practicality when, in fact, the two arguments made contradict each other:

1. That this is a find of no real significance.
2. That the find should be in the care of the British government's chosen representative alone in order to ensure proper handling and classification.

So which is it? Does this uncovered chamber not matter at all, or is it of such importance that a mere woman cannot handle the task of exposing it? It is the very hypocrisy that lies at the heart of so many men; they want everything their own way, and when I point out the failings in their logic I am told that I am simply not intelligent enough to understand it. They speak their private language of power, and I am not afraid to point out that it is often gibberish.

Doctor Morrowley arrived just before the sun had unleashed its midday heat, with a large caravan of workers in tow. Luckily, we were prepared for him. The camels kicked up a cloud of sand that Waleed had spotted on the horizon, so we were able to hide some of the smaller pieces within our tent – but moving the sarcophagus itself was out of the question. So, with the greatest of reluctance, I left Khefatra in her resting place and emerged to greet the Doctor directly.

I have already recorded my thoughts on the theories and practices of Doctor Morrowley. I will not repeat them here except to illustrate them with today's example of his failure to comprehend the significance of my find. He insisted upon entering the chamber without my presence, and when he emerged, heaved back into the now sweltering sunlight by a team of his own workers, he immediately took out a notebook and pen and began to list the artefacts he had spotted within. I stood behind him and watched, over his shoulder, as he wrote his inventory. All he had seen by the light of his lamp was what could be taken – not what should be cherished.

His attention was, of course, fixed on the great death mask. I could tell from the way his hand shook as he wrote of it that he knew it was a miraculous find.

The sarcophagus itself, he listed as such:

Casing (engraved with symbols) that contains a wrapped figure.

I need write no more.

I tapped his shoulder and waited for him to put away his notebook and pen before informing him of who she was, and how I had come across her resting place through my arduous study of many years. He replied that he had no time for 'emotional theories' and would look to ascertain the identity of the corpse after crating it and moving it to the Egyptian Antiquities Museum, as already agreed between the two governments.

At that point I will admit I abandoned any pretence of civility. I begged him not to treat her in such a fashion, and he called for smelling salts so I should not be 'overcome by hysteria'.

Ever faithful Waleed then escorted me back to my tent while Nigel attempted to reason with the man. I sit here awaiting the outcome of their negotiations; I can hear them speaking in their reasonable tones. I already know I cannot bear to lose the one thing Morrowley will demand. He leaves me with no choice.

~

17ᵗʰ April

I have done something so profoundly antithetical to my nature that I cannot quite believe it. I feel weakened by my own actions; I can no longer claim strength through my moral impregnability.

I am on a ship, bound for London.

Money changed hands to arrange my transport at such short notice; I did not see how much. And then I bade goodbye to Waleed. We parted dockside, and he must run. He will be blamed and hunted for my actions until such time as I can clear his name, and I will owe him a great debt forever more that I cannot hope to pay.

I am both a thief, and a desecrator of the one thing I have always purported to love.

If there had been any way to take Khefatra's

body with me, I would have done so. But how could I possibly move her? I am but one woman, travelling alone, and that in itself draws suspicious eyes. To then commandeer enough porters to move a crate big enough to contain her – no. Besides, I could not have brought her up from the darkness. I will leave that to Morrowley. No doubt he has already done so, if he has not decided to pursue the mask himself.

I must hope that he has swallowed the story we concocted. I will not know if this has worked until Nigel writes to me. Will a letter from him beat me back to England? Perhaps, if it travels on one of the newer, faster ships. My own journey will take at least two weeks, with a stopover in Lisbon. I must be patient. I can use this time to make my observations about the mask, which currently sits within my trunk, beside me here in this cabin. I heard the porters complain of the weight after they had delivered it to me: 'Women and their baggage!' Such common assumptions about my affection for material possessions over knowledge will allow me to hide in plain sight, so I shall not take offence this time.

And now to work. I shall immerse myself in

the mask to make the time pass, and my doubts shall disperse. I am the same as I always was! Yes. I will stay the same. Work will make me so.

~

18 April

Looking back over these pages, I realise I will have to record my recent actions more fully. I cannot escape them, and I will not justify them: that would be an act of moral cowardice. I can only write down what happened that night, and hope to find some future understanding within it.

On the night following the arrival of Doctor Morrowley to the excavation site, my mind would not be stilled. As I lay beside my gently snoring Nigel, I noted how my breath erupted from my mouth in plumes, and then dispersed in the cold tent. In, out, in, out: breathing, the act of survival to which we are all bound. Khefatra did not breathe any more; she had no care for the worries of this world. I almost envied her.

Then I heard a voice. It was, unmistakeably, the voice of my mother, close to my left ear, as if she crouched beside the bed, her mouth by my pillow.

We will only be given what we can each bear to carry.

I do not think of my mother often. She was an uneventful woman who eschewed meaningful conversation for endless platitudes, and I soon learned to cease listening when she spoke to me. From quite a young age I craved only the company of my father, and awaited his return from his latest expedition so he could tell me stories of his adventures throughout the dark continent. What a mark he made upon the world. A mighty river bears his name proudly – as did I until my marriage. In a curious way I was glad to leave the surname of Templeton behind and step out from his long shadow to begin my own adventures as Mrs Ursula Carleton. Although he had been dead for many years before my wedding, I still felt his presence and even thought to hear his strong, deep voice at times.

Why, then, would it be my mother who whispered to me?

I can think of no reason. We did not grow closer after his death. She had not been strong to start with, and his absence seemed to diminish her further. Her only interest became the regular visits of friends, colleagues and followers of my father who asked to stand in his office and leaf through his numerous diaries. She would invite them to stay to tea, and then regale them with his stories, mixed with a heavy dose of her own moral idioms, which embarrassed me greatly.

She died quietly three years ago, slipping away in her sleep: an end that suited her. I have not missed her sayings from that day to this.

We will only be given what we can each bear to carry.

It was, indeed, a phrase she might say. Meaningless when examined closely, except... except this time I understood it. It was a veiled command of a kind my mother would never have dared to utter. Did I misunderstand her throughout my life, or had some creature taken her voice and used it to propel me forward? All I can write is that I felt certain that I needed to rise, to dress, and to slip from the tent to step between the sleeping workers on the sand until I found Waleed, roused him, and bade him to lower me into the chamber.

Darkness is darkness; it is not possible to find a colour beyond the utter black that dominates where the sun's rays no longer penetrate, and yet somehow the burial chamber, that night, seemed blacker than ever before. I clutched the handle of my lamp and thrust it before me, but it could not banish the fear that I felt. The eyes of the Gods were upon me from where they had been painted on the walls so many years ago: Horus, Heqet, Thoth and Anubis watched me fumble my way to the sarcophagus, clumsy in terror, and reach out for the death mask of Khefatra.

I knew it would be heavy, but I soon found there was no method by which I could carry both the mask and the lamp. Eventually I gathered all my courage and abandoned the lamp, leaving the warm circle of its light as I edged back to the sling with the mask filling my arms, its grotesque features turned up to mine.

With the last of my strength I managed to position the mask within the sling; Waleed then hauled on the rope. Up went the great treasure, and there followed minutes of agonising silence before the sling descended once more. Silence? Not quite. I must be honest. I thought I heard my mother's voice again, faintly, emanating from the far wall that bore the painting of Heqet.

Bear to carry

An echo, perhaps? I imagined her retreating, sinking back into the wall, turning away from me, and I found within me an intense desire to chase her and ask her, just this once, to speak plainly. I think I would have done so, but for the lowering at that moment of the sling once more. Waleed called my name, once, with urgency, and I positioned myself within so he could pull me up from the chamber.

When I returned to the tent, Nigel was awake and nearly dressed, putting on his boots to come in search of me. I explained my plan: to abscond with the mask and complete the examination of it within my own time, to then better repudiate Morrowley's half-baked theories.

"Bold," he said. "Too bold." I wondered then if I had finally asked too much of him. Then he smiled, and said, "It's worthy of a man. You never will accept less than that, will you?"

I said, "Never," and kissed him.

He then honed the details, persuading me that it would make sense for him to stay behind and blame a worker for the theft of the mask, then offer to work alongside Morrowley, thereby keeping our enemy close. My own sudden absence could then be explained as a resurgence of a hysterical issue needing the care of my personal physician. No gentleman could question such an occurrence.

I miss Nigel terribly already – and Waleed, also. My right hand man. Poor Waleed. But he assured me he can hide away and remain free until the truth can be told. How brave he is. I must do honour to his sacrifice by working hard to find my answers from the mask. Let this task commence immediately!

~

22 April

Over dinner Captain Braylock enquired after my health. I thanked him for his concern and attempted to eat a little more of my lamb chop, which was on the fatty side. Just writing of it now makes my stomach clench; I abandoned it when I could stand no more, and was aware of his puzzlement as I hurried from the table.

I had hoped that claiming mal-de-mer would allow me to be left to my own devices within my cabin in the main, which is small but adequate for my needs. In truth, I have felt terribly nauseous; the sea is rough, and the sky is so very overcast and gloomy whenever I venture out on deck. But it is not only the weather than unsettles me so. It is the mask, and the messages it contains within.

Of course I was expecting to find carvings on the interior of the mask. That could hardly come as a surprise to any self-respecting Egyptologist. But just as the visage is unusual, possibly unique, so the Hieratic used within conveys a message unlike anything I have seen.

The symbols are tiny, and they are numerous. Every inch of the interior surface is covered, and in places there is even overlapping to the point of unintelligibility – how could anyone translate these scorings in entirety, ranging from deep gashes to the lightest of pressures, made in a hand that ranges from violent outbursts to the tenderest of care?

Do I really believe that this is the work of one writer? I do. There are clear similarities in the strokes; a voice reaches through the dark centuries, shouting, whispering, begging me to understand.

A day's work revealed one small phrase to me. One phrase, from so many, carved above the right eye socket, and the act of translation revealed more than the words themselves. It connected me once more to that eerie occurrence on the night of the theft, in a way that I cannot begin to comprehend:

Tears and smiles can come together

This is the exact phrase my mother often said to those who visited the house after the death of my father. A weak platitude that was one of her personal favourites, she bored me incessantly with it. I have checked my translation many times over.

I hear both my mother's voice and an older, wiser presence when I read these markings. Which is to be believed? Or am I simply imagining both? I must press on.

Sea air, it seems, is not conducive to a clear head after all.

~

24 April

It's not the air that is to blame at all. It is my own body. To create life whilst I was in the midst of studying an ancient, long-dead world... I have always looked only to the past, and now I must look forward instead.

I cannot begin to record how I feel about this event because I simply do not know myself. I veer wildly from excitement to despair, which shames me. Surely I should be delight itself with such news? Is this not what a woman is made for?

And yet the truth is I have never quite felt like a woman.

I will write Nigel a letter telling him of our news as soon as I return home. I wish I could see the pride in his eyes as he learns of our news, and allow that pride to infect me. But the thought of it will be enough. Yes, I can be happy at Nigel's joy.

Captain Braylock insisted upon the doctor conducting an examination for my sea sickness, and I am now glad that he did so even though at the time I was filled with irritation, and protested. "You must be taken care of," he said. I loathe such sentiments but perhaps, this time, he was right. The doctor enquired after certain private issues and then told me of the baby.

The baby.

He is a young man with a charming yet professional manner, and he tells me I am at least three months along! I simply did not consider it. I lost track of all time in the desert; besides that, I had never had a concern for such issues. Well, now I must begin to do so. I do not think I would have noticed my condition for more months to come; I am so unobservant about such matters.

~

26 April

It transpires that it is extremely difficult to sit around like a Bakewell pudding and think of nothing but the welfare of one's internal passenger.

During the stopover at Lisbon yesterday the Coddings (a dear old couple celebrating their anniversary) insisted upon keeping me company on board while others disembarked to see the castle. It was deemed for too adventurous for me; I was informed of this is a low voice by Mrs Codding, who informed me that everyone had been told of my condition in order to ensure that I am taken care of properly at all times.

We played nothing but three-handed cribbage for hours – hours that I could have spent working.

But I must confess, I continue to work when I cannot be monitored by others. I hate to tell untruths to such well-meaning souls as the Coddings, but what they do not know cannot hurt them. So, while crew and passengers sleep, I work as if my life depends upon it. I simply cannot change my nature – and, what's more, I have come to the conclusion that to do so would be detrimental to my health and therefore also to the health of my baby. I know Nigel would agree with me on this matter.

Onwards. I made progress last night, and think I will have translated the long phrase over the left eye by dawn tomorrow.

~

27 April

It cannot be right.

I must start again. I mistranslate – no. It would be better to start again.

She glowers at me so. She whispers in my mother's voice. I am disappointing her.

~

28 April

Damn them all! Why can they not give me a moment to myself? I cannot think with the Coddings forever hovering outside my cabin door.

I will be so glad to see Southampton; there will be transport awaiting me for Sussex, and once I am within the four walls of my library I will be able to concentrate on what has occurred.

But there is no doubt that I cannot do good work here, and I am making terrible errors: errors in translation, and in judgement.

I will return the mask to my trunk, and try to remain calm until I can unpack it in peace.

~

1 May

I only think of her expression. That terrible grimace. Why? Why, combined with such words? She haunts me.

The steward has just knocked on the door; we have docked. Disembarkation is commencing.

The curse comes for me. I do not feel well. I fear for my thoughts. I fear for my child: what is within me? I fear it is she. Surely it is she.

~

— Part Two —

20 September

The mask is deciphered, and I am myself again.

I am uncomfortable for much of the time. I have grown so large, and will become larger still, but I find my mind has a clarity once more that it has lacked for many months. I feel an optimism for the new task awaiting me: motherhood. I wish to excel at it – to raise a person of character who will make their own mark upon the world. Yes, now I have ensured the remembrance of Khefatra, and my own undeniable abilities as an Egyptologist, explorer and translator, I will look less to the past and give my all to the future instead.

It is good to write of my personal thoughts once more. I did not dare, for a while. Not while

Doctor Sanding – an old friend of Nigel's – watched me so closely, looking for signs of increased agitation, for I am certain he would have insisted upon reading every word within this journal if he had known of it. I hid it away and worked only upon my translation in the hours they allotted to me. Thank goodness for Nigel's intervention by letter – it was only his insistence that refusing to allow me to work would exacerbate my unrest that persuaded the good doctor to allocate me two hours of time in my library every day.

On the subject of letters: I wrote to Nigel this morning and included the first translation of the Hieratic with instructions for him to pass it to Morrowley, and reveal that the mask is safe and within our possession. This is my bargaining chip; I know Nigel will play it wisely. The translation itself is a most enlightening and informative document. I will admit only here that I have taken the liberty of omitting the sections that reminded me of my mother's advice. Although I dreaded finding more such snippets, in fact I found only two – one above each eye socket – and I have decided that it was only my ever-busy brain at work, making vague connections that later came to be obvious. For it is true, although I could never have rationally foreseen it, that both my mother and Khefatra were supplanted and diminished. Belittled by their own choices. By the very men they loved.

I have come to realise that my mother would have been quite a different woman without the influence of my father upon her. He was always the centre of our lives, and he enjoyed that position immensely. But I now understand that becoming a satellite to another extols a high price. It sucks the colour and vivacity from one's being. I, for instance, could not even begin to reach my potential until I had moved from my father's sphere of influence. In the case of my mother, she lost sense of who she was if she was not part of him. I did not know her at all; the person I knew was only part of the shadow cast by my father: she became nothing more than a living ghost of the girl she had been.

But what of Khefatra? How could a Pharaoh have been but a ghost?

The mask gave me my long-sought answers. It is clear that she was one of the children of Ptolemy XII. Upon his death she acceded to the rule of Egypt, and she commanded the might and wealth of that nation for six years, alone, which is a magnificent achievement. The usual path was for a female ruler to be married to a male sibling to consolidate power, but the scribe of the mask is definite that no such union happened. In fact, the deaths of her siblings is recorded – the cause of death? I can only speculate.

There then followed a period of prosperity, described as 'blessings from Heqet'. Heqet was the goddess of fertility and childbirth; did Khefatra give birth, then? Have many children of her own, without a husband? What an astonishing thought.

At that point, the mask records, Khefatra appointed a chief consort. She did not take a husband; the scribe is clear on this point. But powers are given to the consort, who is highly favoured. Perhaps she loves him. He grows stronger, even as Khefatra begins to weaken. 'Heqet withdraws her gifts': that is how this weakness is described. I hazard a guess that Khefatra's fertility has ended – through illness, or through natural changes in the body? There are so many aspects to her life that we will never uncover.

The consort moves against her. He seizes power for himself.

She is taken away. If she did have children before he became her chosen partner, they were removed too. Probably murdered. Not even their names remain.

The consort becomes ruler supreme. He takes the name Ptolemy XIII and he erases as much information as he can that might reveal he is not a rightful king. He obliterates written records of Khefatra wherever he can, and has dates changed to show that he was the natural successor and child of Ptolemy XII.

She is, at least, granted a proper Egyptian burial.

Was, I should write. She was. How peculiar. It seemed to me that all of these acts were, through the act of writing, suddenly contemporaneous with my own existence. But now, finally, her story is told. And it can be told again, and again, and again.

One thing still troubles me: why was her death mask so grotesque? I cannot think she was disfigured in life; that, surely, would have stopped all hope of her accession to power. Men do not, I think, take orders from ugly women.

What does that twisted countenance represent?

~

6 October

I anxiously await a reply from Nigel. The only cure is to devote my time and energy to my growing child, which I have done with fervour, and found so many aspects of our mutual existence that I did not notice before.

It is the strangest of blessings to make such a connection to another human being whom I cannot yet see or touch. They are ensconced with their own private world that just happens to be part of me. But we communicate: I know so much about them already. The lazy shifts to and fro in the hours of darkness, as if trying to find a comfortable spot; the bouts of hiccups if I happen to eat too much kedgeree in the morning; the tiny foot that extends so far that I can see its outline through my stretched skin: all of these details create a character.

They create my nascent girl.

Do I dare to write that? Only to and for

myself. It is my deep, unspoken belief that I carry a female child, who will embody the spirit of the women I have long admired. Something powerful is being passed down through me. I have not even mentioned this to my husband, who has now been away for so long that our letters no longer contain any aspects of marital intimacy.

Will I be disappointed if my instincts are proven wrong? I do not know. I suspect so, and I am aware that is a terrible admission but that is only because I already feel as if I know this little woman, waiting to emerge at the right moment. She, I think, will know when.

~

8 October

Such excitement! I have heard from Nigel, and he writes that he has explained all to Morrowley and brokered a marvellous deal on the strength of my translation. It is – and Nigel says Morrowley is in agreement with this – a hugely important find.

I always knew it would be so. And I know, now, that it was absolutely the correct course of action to leave Nigel to these negotiations. It was a situation that needed to be handled man to man. All I need do is dispatch the mask to the Museum in Cairo, where Nigel and Morrowley are to address other scholars and announce the find. If only I could make that journey and present my findings myself! But no, no, my baby's safety compels me to stay here. Doctor Sanding is adamant that any journey is not to be undertaken.

Only a few weeks remain until she comes, I think.

I feel so very sleepy, and I move from room to room arranging cushions and fretting at nothing. *Nesting* – says my housekeeper, who has been a boon in many ways, but does annoy me somewhat with her inconsequential conversation on issues such as her nieces and nephews. Why do women assume that all members of their kind will be fascinated by tales of unrelated offspring? I hope I do not snub her too obviously, but really, my patience is wearing very thin.

Now, I must get the mask wrapped and prepared. It has been sitting on my library desk for many months now, in front of a mirror that

I have used to view both front and back simultaneously during my research. I shall hope to get it dispatched today. The desk will seem quite empty without it.

~

1 November

This cannot be right. But I have read the article twice. This cannot be right.

There are pains, low in the belly. The doctor has been summoned by the housekeeper. She says not to write, but I must, I must record what has happened, to try to make sense of it, to understand why

~

3 November

I am a mother.

I do not recognise this child: my daughter. She is not the spirit of others, embodied. She is herself. Apart from me. She is only herself.

Perhaps there can be relief in that.

~

The housekeeper says I should sleep if the baby is sleeping, but that is very difficult to do with these emotions trapped within me.

Joy – isn't that common? A rush of personal fulfilment? A deep sense of care, and unconditional love: maternal emotions. I do not have them.

I have had the crib moved to the library so I can write as she sleeps, and to see her arms and legs pulled in to her tiny body, her delicate chest rising and falling, only makes me frightened for her. She does not know what kind of world she enters.

She comes to a world where men with little conscience thrive while good men are punished. And there is no place in this world for women at all.

I am not certain that my husband is a good man any more.

He must answer my letter. He must explain the article in the *Times*. The find of the century: yes. That I can agree with. Attributed to Mr Carleton and Doctor Morrowley: no. This is so far from the truth that it can only be deliberate.

What will Nigel tell me? Will he say that Morrowley refused to believe a woman was capable of this work? We have been too long apart if he thinks I will accept such an explanation. If only I could see his face. I must try to comprehend it. And dear Waleed, ever faithful. How could Nigel have let harm come to him?

But in the name of honesty I must record how my own conscience pricks over the issue of Waleed. I was so very selfish to let him take the blame for my theft of the mask. I had thought this issue could be easily sorted; how could I have believed that?

This is also my fault.

~

18 November

There is still no word from Nigel. Although my letter will not have reached him yet, he will have received the telegraph informing him of the birth of our child and has had ample time to reply. Besides the arrival of his daughter, should he not have raced to explain the article to me as soon as it was published?

I have written to him many times since then: several times a day. I had been attempting to hold my temper, thinking that vexing him with accusations will not help the situation. Enough of that. Let him be vexed as I am. Let him read my grievances, and be struck by them as I am continually struck anew by the passages of the article I cannot forget:

'Mr Carleton and Doctor Morrowley expressed relief to have the magnificent golden burial mask in their care once more following its theft by a local miscreant, who has since been caught and dealt with severely.'

Or:

'The mask will remain at the Museum of Egyptian Antiquities, Cairo, for further examination by the pair. As it is an unprepossessing sight, Morrowley suggests that it is not a sight for the faint-hearted and may never be placed on public display.'

This paragraph causes me the most grievous pain:

'Both experts are in agreement that the mask came from the tomb of one of the wives of Ptolemy XIII, and will therefore offer great insight into his prosperous reign.'

So they have not only supplanted my rightful place, but also obliterated Khefatra's name once more.

The baby wakes; I must put down my pen and attend.

~

20 November

Finally, a letter arrives. It is filled with tender, unconvincing words. Exactly as I thought, Nigel writes that Morrowley and the other scholars would have it no other way.

'What was I to do?' he writes. 'At least this way the Carleton name remains upon the discovery.'

For the first time I realise Carleton is his name, not mine.

Then he writes of his delight at receiving the telegram informing him of the birth of our daughter. He asks if she could be named Isabella, after his own dear mother.

I do not know who she is, but she is no Isabella. She is awake beside me, in her crib, opening and closing her hands; her attention is on the afternoon light through the long windows. She makes small sounds of contentment. I would rather she had no name at all than be given a ridiculous one, only to then have it forgotten.

The housekeeper has been fretting at this, I know. She knocked on the door earlier and begged me to get some rest. She said she would take care of the child, and did I not have a name for the poor little one yet? I shouted at her to leave, and set the baby crying. No doubt she will be summoning Doctor Sanding once more as I write.

~

28 November

I am decided. I cannot sit by any longer. I will go to Nigel and have my explanations in person, and the baby will come with me.

No more lies. His latest letter is unbearable. He says he has received a telegraph from the doctor, and he is worried for my health. He suggests finding a good nurse and leaving the baby so I can recuperate in a sanatorium.

If I am ill, Nigel, it is because you have made me this way! Enough writing. I have told the housekeeper to get the trunk brought down from the attic.

~

My name is Ursula Carleton née Templeton. I am an Egyptologist and an adventuress. My daughter is a fine and happy baby in my care. She manages to sleep at this moment, even through the racket in the hall. Doctor Sanding shouts that he has my husband's permission to intervene for the good of the child, and he is summoning the gardeners to help him knock down the library door. I have a few more minutes, then.

I now understand that Khefatra's curse is real.

I recognise the grotesque expression upon her death mask. I have just seen that expression. I catch sight of it in the mirror that sits upon my desk, upon my very own face, as I realise what is about to happen to me.

The twisted, open mouth and the thick lines around the nose and wide eyes: this is the face a woman makes when they take everything away from her. This is the face a mother makes before the child is pulled out of her arms. I hear more voices. The men will begin the task of breaking down the door, and the baby will wake and cry. I will cajole her, and tell her tears and smiles can come together. I hear my mother's voice again, moving through me. I cannot escape her. I am the ugly, screaming face inside – the men are at the

~

Author's Afterword

In 2015 a minute examination of Tutankhamen's famous death mask revealed remains of a cartouche. The name that had been erased by Egyptian artisans was that of a woman: Ankhkheperure Neferneferuaten. Some experts believe the mask was originally made for a female Egyptian ruler, possibly Nefertiti. There is evidence to suggest Nefertiti ruled Egypt as Pharaoh after the death of her husband, Akhenaten (who made her co-regent during his reign). Why her mask should have been taken and her name erased from it remains a mystery.

A Very Modern Monster

My father told me that George would sometimes come down to the Forest Inn on an evening. It was near Simonsbath, in the heart of Exmoor, and wasn't the rustic place I was expecting, but a gastropub with a string of lights across the windows, and a busy car park. The moor had become a tourist destination for those on the hunt for an unspoiled slice of England. But no matter what kind of establishment was erected in it, it retained its character: the clouds brooded over the clumps of grasses and bogs, the gorse squatted on the roots of the blackthorn, and the dampness pervaded. It was not beautiful; its image could not have been used to sell you something. But it definitely was unspoiled. When I walked upon it, for the first time in years, I did not have the feeling that I had left footprints. No mark, no path. It was disinterested in my presence.

For five days I waited at the Forest Inn, eating well, choosing the seats between the open fire and the largest window, so I could see over the moor. It was red, the colour of autumn, the moss rusting in the rain. I worried that I would not recognise George but as soon as he walked through the door – on my last day, the Thursday – I knew him. He was the same; the uncle who appeared rarely at family gatherings, and who brought a sense of unease into the room with him. He looked around the pub with the air of a man checking for enemies, and then his eyes fell on me. I raised a hand, and he cocked his head, then strolled to the bar and talked to the woman working there. I thought for a moment I would have to go over to him and introduce myself, but after paying for his pint he sauntered over to my table, and gave me a quizzical, penetrating stare that made me feel twenty years younger.

'Uncle George,' I said.

He pointed a finger at me. 'Eve. Is that right?'

I nodded.

'I knew it. You look just like your mother.'

'Mum's dead,' I said, and could say no more.

He sat down beside me and patted my hand as I struggled for control. He hated people and their emotional displays; he was famous in the family for it, and I had been determined not to put him in the situation where he had to comfort me. So much for that.

'What was it?' he asked, after a few minutes of silence.

'A stroke.'

'Ahhhh…' He shook his head. 'Poor Becky. Poor Becky. How's your Dad taking it?'

'We're all doing the best we can.'

His only sister had died and he took it well. I've always wondered about that phrase, taking death well, as if it's a pill to be swallowed, after which all symptoms will clear up. There is no way to take it well, is there? It can't be conquered simply by acting equably in its presence.

'Have you buried her yet?' he said. The directness of it took me back for a moment.

'This Saturday. I've been hoping to see you, to let you know. Can you come?'

'Of course, of course,' he said, and I gave him the details. We didn't discuss how he would get there, or where he would stay. Instead he asked me about my life up in Bristol, whether I liked my job as a Graphic Designer, if there were any young men on the scene. He said how Mum had written him long letters and sent them to the pub; I could picture her doing that. I wondered what she had told him. Then he got up to leave with only a wink in my direction, and the promise of seeing me again that Saturday.

After he left, I felt the eyes of the woman who worked behind the bar upon me. Eventually she came over to clear away his glass, and asked me if I was all right. It seemed being in my Uncle's presence brought out a secretive, taciturn side of my personality. I told her I was fine, and let her reach her own conclusions. It was nobody's business but mine. But I was surprised by her interest; it did not feel like a casual question. In the way she held my gaze, I could have sworn I saw a warning.

~

I was aware of George, standing behind me, as they cremated my mother. He had been a boy once, a boy fond of toy guns and running around in the Devon woods. The boy grew into a soldier. Special Forces, the kind of soldier who does the dirty jobs and never speaks of it. He would emerge from that life every now and again, his thin lips pressed so tightly together in the shadow of his peppery beard.

I remembered my birthday party, on the year he turned up out of the blue with a deep tan, and a large rectangular present. It turned out to be a board game, something cheerful, with a picture of a smiling family with very white teeth on the lid. He didn't stay long, that day. He never did. I asked Mum why, and she said, 'Your uncle can't be around people.' Soon after that he got pensioned off, and returned to Devon. I think he had a house for a while, but then his furniture arrived at our home in a large van, and I was told he had decided to live on the moor. 'It will suit him better,' said Mum. 'He can take care of himself.'

'But what about the Beast?' I asked. The Beast of Exmoor was a big deal back then. Sheep were regularly being found with their throats ripped out, and a loping creature, lithe and black, had been seen, swishing a long, sinuous tail. A puma, escaped from a zoo, the other kids at school said, copying the overheard conversations of their parents.

My mother laughed. 'Trust me, if the Beast comes across Uncle George, it had better run the other way. Fast.'

The coffin finished its slow journey through the red velvet curtains, and the cremation came to an end. Dad and I stood by the stone arched doorway of the chapel, shaking hands and kissing cheeks to a soft background of Mozart.

Uncle George was the last to leave. Dad was busy talking to Mum's old manager from the office she worked at, so George had me all to himself. Looking back on it, I think that was what he had been waiting for.

'Thanks for coming,' I said, holding out my hand, and he grasped me by the wrist.

'Come visit me,' he said. 'I'll show you the moor, proper. I'll show you why I came back to it and your mother went far away from it.'

'That's very kind,' I said. 'I, um, have a lot on, but maybe...'

He shook his head. 'Not a holiday. Not an obligation.' He formed the words with distaste. 'If you want to see something truthful, then come. Bring a sleeping bag. That's all you'll need.'

I pulled my hand back; he let me go, and winked.

'Well, thanks again,' I said, and Dad turned to us and echoed my words, and I was freed from George's intensity. A few minutes later, and he had gone. The service was over. I put away my black suit at the back of the wardrobe and returned to work, fully expecting to never see him again.

But every now and again his offer popped into my mind, as I was working on a project, or doing the shopping, steering my trolley down the long rows of brightly coloured products, trying to choose between thirty types of breakfast cereal. Red packets, green packets, yellow packets: it brought to mind the eternal browns of Exmoor, the browns of the earth, the simplest of all colours. The moor had rolled away from the window of the Forest Inn, in all directions, the same, no matter where I looked.

It was the beginning of December. I set out on a trip into town to buy Christmas presents, and found myself standing in a camping shop, asking the assistant what kind of sleeping bag would be best for a trip to Exmoor.

'In December?' he asked. 'You'd better go heavy duty.' And he loaded me up with thermals, stout walking boots, a serious rucksack, a torch, a flask, a compass, even a small stove and mess tins. By the time he had finished I felt like a soldier myself.

~

George took great pleasure in examining the items in my rucksack. We sat side by side in his battered campervan, on a sofa that could fold out to make an extra bed, and he marvelled at each gadget. 'Amazing,' he said. 'Did you think you were going to be out here without a scrap of shelter?'

'I didn't know.'

'I've got Calor Gas, you know. Even a hot shower. The ranger turns a blind eye to me being out here, although I have to move the van on every now and again, just for appearances. I'm mainly here or out Oare way though. You know Oare? Where Lorna Doone was shot? Lots of old stories around these parts. Coffee? You can make it on your little stove here if you like, but I've got a kettle.'

'Lovely.' I started to repack my rucksack as he

lit his gas ring with a match, and busied about with cups.

'Right about now you must be wondering what you're doing here,' he said. I didn't reply. It was late, the darkness total, pressing against the windows. When I walked into the Inn he had already been there, eating roast turkey from the Christmas menu, looking for all the world as if he was there to meet me. 'I can show you some owls in the morning. You'll hear them, tonight, screeching. Barn owls, that is. They screech and Tawnies toowhit-toowhoo. Screech like someone being murdered, they do. I'll show you them sleeping tomorrow. And the deer, they get so cocky out here, come right up to the door of the van. No people for miles, see, not enough of humanity for them to learn to be scared of us. There's sheep, of course, not all fluffy like in the picture books but wild things, tangled and dirty. The gorse bushes are like giant balls of cotton where their wool gets caught on the thorns. Crows get their eyes, sometimes, you find them blind and wandering, like beggars from the bible. And then there's mutton for tea.'

He placed the coffee in front of me, black, like syrup. Everything here was different. An old question popped into my mind. 'What about the Beast?' I said.

'What about it?'

'Is it still...out here?'

'So you believe in the Beast?' he said.

'I thought it was an escaped animal. A big cat.'

He took down a packet of biscuits from an overhead cupboard and offered them to me. 'It's been forty years now. How long do big cats live, can you tell me that?' I would have searched for the answer on my phone, but there was no reception. 'Thirteen years. And that's the longest, not taking into account these freezing winters, the climate here. No, it's not just an animal.'

'What is it, then?'

He smiled at me. 'A monster.'

Was he serious? I couldn't tell. My mother's words came back to me, about how he couldn't be around people. Or maybe they shouldn't be around him. He was my Uncle, a blood relative; he had brought me presents, once upon a time. But, with his blue eyes fixed on mine, his white beard sticking out from his chapped face, there was something wild about him. Dangerous.

'Stop pulling my leg,' I said, and he laughed.

'Just like your mother,' he said, and the moment passed. He brought out some playing cards. The only game we both knew was Blackjack, and we played it for hours. He delighted in slapping down his cards on the wobbly table, shouting, making the van rock. I began to enjoy myself, as he told stories of his childhood, even of the places he had visited: the Middle East, Africa. There was never any mention of the job he had been there to do. He made it sound like a series of holidays, and I wondered what he was leaving out for my benefit. Or perhaps he really had forgotten the reality of it during his years spent out on the moor. How disconnected had he become?

'There are monsters all over those places,' George said, as he dealt a fresh hand. 'Legends, stories, the local kids grow up on them, and there's no doubt in their minds that those monsters are real. Ancient, and real. It's easier to believe in something when it's been around for so long, do you think? Like Jesus. Like God himself.' He gave a dry cough of a laugh. 'Haven't you ever wondered what it was like when that monster was brand new to the world? They all have to start out little, and grow, don't you think?'

'There's no room for monsters in the modern world,' I told him. 'No place where there could be dragons any more. Everything is explored, and mapped. Satellite technology.'

'Really?' He pointed out of the window. 'It won't help you out there. You might be able to see it from space, but when you're on your own two feet, on the moor, in winter, you're only a few bad choices from death, and they maybe won't find your frozen body to stick in a coffin for the sake of a fancy ceremony, with your relatives gathered around. If the cold doesn't take you, the Beast will. Blackjack!' He smacked down his cards, delighted.

Eventually he lost enthusiasm for both the game and the subject, and we folded down the sofa to make an extra bed. He took off only his boots before crawling under his duvet; I thought of my clean thermal pyjamas, brand new, in my rucksack. But I didn't want to change clothes in that tiny van, not in front of him. It would feel like letting down my defences. So I removed my own boots, and slid into my sleeping bag, smelling the newness of it, hearing it crackle as I moved.

George turned off the light and, within moments, started to snore. It was comical, a rich, deep sound, and it took my mind away from the things he had said, and the blackness of the moor, separated from me by only the thin wall of the campervan. I listened to him, smiled in the dark, and controlled my breathing: in, out, in, out. Sleep stole over me, and I was glad that the Beast didn't follow me into my dreams.

~

A scream.

No – a screech. George had told me of the barn owls. They sounded so loud, so close. I lay in the utter black, cocooned in my sleeping bag, feeling the freezing air on my lips and forehead. George made no sound. It seemed he could sleep through anything.

As the owls screeched on, the suspicion began to grow in me that he wasn't sleeping at all.

I groped for my rucksack and silently thanked the sales assistant for suggesting the pencil torch; it was clipped to the flap of my rucksack. The beam was a pinpoint of intense white light that trembled with my hand as I swung it over the gas ring, the cupboard, to his bed.

It was empty.

Fear pressed against my ribs, squeezed my throat. My eyes stung with the struggle to see clearly in the torchlight – was that a movement, under the duvet? But how could it be? No, everything was still, and I was alone. Miles from anything I knew. I told myself he must have simply gone out for a walk. The torchlight found no trace of his boots. Yes, a walk. He was unpredictable, a law to himself. A man with a fondness for monsters.

The owls fell silent. They must have flown away, hunting for the small, scurrying voles and mice that ran from sedge to gorse, crouching low.

Then I heard it – a low hum. It moved along the length of the campervan, around the front, towards the door. I snapped off the torch and burrowed deep into the sleeping bag, willing myself into stillness. The hum grew, became a rough, grating sound, as loud and insistent as machinery, and I pictured – what? A monster:

teeth, eyes, claws, hardness, heaviness, every terrible imagining that had ever grabbed me and forced itself into my head. This was no escaped cat. It was a living nightmare.

And it was at the door.

I lay still. So still. I listened to it, and I felt it listen for me. I saw, in my mind, velvet black ears, twitching, rotating.

Time ticked on, and it began to move away from the door. The sound lessened, became a soft hum once more, and was gone.

I couldn't move. George didn't come back until the dawn had begun to sneak its rosy fingers into the van, and I pretended to be asleep as he moved around, and got back into bed. After a time, he began to snore once more. Still I didn't sleep. I didn't think I would ever be able to sleep again.

~

Over a breakfast of sausages, bacon and eggs, all jumbled together in a filthy frying pan over the one gas ring, I tried to find the words to tell George that I was leaving.

'A morning out on the moor,' he said, 'that's what you need. There's plenty to see.'

'No, I really think—'

'Stay the morning, and then see what you think come the afternoon. I'll take you back to the Forest Inn myself. Well, you won't reach it on your own anyway, will you?' He laughed, and I hated him. The feeling freed my tongue.

'You went out last night.'

'Yes, that I did. I had some business to take care of.'

'What kind of business?'

He tapped his nose.

'There was a sound. Outside the van. A...I can't describe it. Like a hum, that got louder.'

He stopped eating, and put down his knife and fork. 'Is that right?' He cocked his head, and I thought he was considering my words, but then it came to me that he was listening, to the growing sound of a car, coming in our direction. I looked through the window, staring into the morning mist, and a Landover came into view, stuttering over the uneven ground.

'Anderson,' said George. 'Quicker than I was expecting.'

The Landrover came to a halt a few feet away, and a tall, bearded man in a green jacket and a wide-brimmed leather hat got out. He had a capable air about him; he strode around the van with a sense of purpose that appealed to me.

George threw open the door. 'Morning.'

Anderson nodded. 'Val told me you had a lady visitor.'

'You would have thought the tourists would keep her too busy in that pub of hers to pay attention to my comings and goings,' said George. 'This is my niece, Eve. She wanted to see the moor.'

'Is that right? Well, I'm thinking you've been too busy for mischief, then. One of the ponies disappeared last night from the travellers' camp, over by Tarr Steps. No sign of it. But you were here with your niece all night.'

'All night,' said George. 'I don't know how the poor thing put up with my snoring. It must have been the Beast that got that pony.'

'Now, George, don't start that again.'

'You're not the police.' George had a placid tone, but only an idiot would not have found him threatening. 'You're a warden. You shouldn't get yourself involved in these things. You know the travellers will turn this moor into a settlement, given a chance. Keep your nose out, and things will take care of themselves.'

'Will they?' They locked eyes, and then the moment passed, and Anderson turned back to me. 'It was nice to meet you, Miss.' I saw my chance to get away diminishing; I had to speak.

'Could you...give me a lift back to the pub, do you think?'

He raised an eyebrow. 'Of course.'

'Later this afternoon,' said George. 'She means later today. It'll save her a walk back to her car, see. About three?'

Anderson nodded. 'I'll come back for you then. I'll be heading back this way anyway.' And then he turned and walked back to his Landrover, and George shut the door.

'I would have taken you,' he said. 'Right, well, we'll have to get a move on. Put on your boots. It's a walk.'

'To what?'

'Boots.'

I obeyed, and left my half-eaten mess of a breakfast behind as we started out at a brisk pace, into the heart of the moor.

~

'Not far now,' said George. We had been walking for over an hour, without pause. My legs weren't used to such punishment, and the muscles burned, even as the intense cold seared my lungs. The landscape looked the same to me in every direction; there were no landmarks, only an occasional bare tree, the trunks squat, the branches twisted.

'Where are we?' I said.

'Not far from the Tunnel.' It didn't mean anything to me, and I had no choice but to keep up with him. He was my only way back to civilisation. 'I first told your mother that this place existed years ago. It was at one of your birthday parties, I remember. She wasn't best pleased to hear about it. She told me not to come back, but I knew she didn't mean it, not really. She never shut the door on me. She wrote long letters to me, trying to keep me in her life. I think that was because she saw a lot of me in you.'

I pictured that party once more. *Your Uncle can't be around people*, she had said. I never imagined she had told him to go. Had she been scared for me? Of his influence?

'I told her to come and see for herself, and she said I was going mad. Those years out there in the Army, such stress. That's the word she used

– stress. She didn't understand that I loved it. It never caused me one sleepless night. Worry is something for the people with the day jobs, the mortgages, things to lose, the fear of what's out there to take away your hopes and dreams. She'd rather live with the fear than face it. But I say - fear only gets worse when you hide from it. I don't think you should live that way.'

He stopped walking, abruptly, and I realised the ground had begun a gentle sloping downwards that accelerated into a steep valley floor. 'There,' he said. The valley ran, like a crack in the surface of the moor, to rocks, piled high, forming a small cave. It had a man-made look about it, incongruous in this setting.

He started down towards it, and I followed suit, feeling the fear of last night returning to me. There was a strange, sweet smell in the air that intensified as we approached the cave; I realised that, just inside the opening, a body lay – the pony, on its side, legs splayed, the white edges of the ribs visible from where the chest and stomach had been ripped open.

I stopped. George went into the cave, and examined the pony. 'It's not eaten much,' he said. 'Ah well. It'll get round to it later. I wonder why it came out to the van? Maybe it caught your scent, on me.'

'Why...?' I couldn't speak further.

'Why have I brought you here? I want you to understand – I found it when I first came out here, to live. It was so small, back then. I was out this way, looking for the rumoured Beast, and it was lying on the ground, so weak, with a gunshot wound in its side. Just a tiny monster, born of some local news stories, but with my help it got well. And now it gets a little stronger every day. Soon it'll take care of itself. This place needs a proper monster, one to keep the tourists and travellers at bay.'

'You're... making a myth?'

'Oh no,' he said. 'I'm not making anything. It's real. Come in and see.'

He walked into the cave.

I stood outside, wanting to run, not knowing what direction might take me to safety. But part of me wanted to go into that cave. It wanted to see the Beast, to know exactly what slept within, what had come to the van in the night and smelled me out. I moved forward; just a few steps, enough to bring me level with the dead pony. George was just ahead of me. I could make out the broad outline of his back. He had crouched a little; it wasn't a large cave, and I became aware of the way it narrowed and dropped down, further into the ground.

'It's dug itself right down in there,' said George. 'Perhaps it tunnels, with those claws. Could be tunnels all over this moor.'

His voice echoed against the walls of the cave. My eyes began to adjust to the darkness. One more step forward and I was inside, and a new sound came to me – that long, low hum, from the night before. Rhythmic, heavy, it was a feeling, a trembling of the ground, as much as a noise.

'It's asleep,' said George. 'You can just see its back. Look.'

A semi-circular shape jutted from the earth. It could easily have been mistaken for another rock, but then I realised there was a regular pattern to the ridge along the central line; scales, perhaps? They shifted upwards and the humming intensified, for a moment, then lessened.

He held out a hand, hovered over the line of the back, then briefly laid his palm upon it. It shuddered, and I knew I had to get out of that place before it woke. I couldn't bear to see it, to know it. The otherness of it was overwhelming.

I stumbled outside and started back along the valley floor, not caring where I went. I heard George behind me, calling my name, and I didn't slow, but he caught up with me and pulled me to a stop, holding on to my rucksack. I turned, swung out, and he stepped back.

'Hold on, hold on, there's no need to get like that, girl.'

'Take me back,' I said. 'I want to go home.'

'Well you're going the wrong way, then, aren't you? What's got you so angry? It wouldn't hurt you. It's still too small for that yet.'

'You're feeding it. You're taking care of it.'

'And one day it'll be big enough to take care of itself, and this moor, and then no doubt it'll get the better of me.' He smiled. 'That's the law of nature, right there. Not the law of man. I don't know how many people understand the difference, but you do now, don't you?'

'You're crazy. Take me back.'

He gave me a look that I could only describe as disappointment. He had expected better from me. Understanding, perhaps. But I felt nothing for Exmoor, saw no beauty in it. I only wanted to get away, from the cold, the damp, the life and the death of it. If monsters had to exist, I wanted it to be in some far away place that I never had to visit.

He turned and led the way, and I followed after, keeping my distance. It was a long walk, but he never spoke, or even looked back to check I was following. When we reached the campervan, Anderson's Landrover was parked outside, waiting for me, and I packed up my belongings without another word to my Uncle. If my mother had ever thought that I was like him, then she had been wrong. I had left Devon when I was still so young. There was nothing left of the earth of Exmoor in me.

~

It was over a year later when a policeman rang to tell me Uncle George had disappeared.

'The Warden reported him missing a few days ago,' said the kindly voice. It had a trace of the Devonian accent, such a soft sound. 'We found his campervan, and everything was untouched. We think maybe he just wandered off and couldn't find his way back. We're still searching, but the chances of finding him now are very slim.'

'You won't find him,' I said.

After that, I kept an eye on the news from the Exmoor region. Ponies ripped apart, found in pieces, partially eaten. A member of a camping expedition went missing, and it was blamed on the bad weather. Then, just last week, a man disappeared, and it made the national news. His car was found near the Forest Inn, with dents and long scratches in the side panels. The papers dug up all those old rumours about a Beast.

I suppose that will happen a lot more often, now.

Afterword

Zombies, vampires, mummies, and the big bad wolf have long been some of my favourite monsters, found first in fairy tales and then on the TV screen late at night, courtesy of Hammer and Amicus and Universal, to name a few. I've loved writing about all of them for this collection. The field gets rounded out with a tale of the Beast of Exmoor, who regularly got talked about at my school when I was a young child in North Devon. He was a very local and modern monster for me. I grew up with him. I think it shows.

Also by Aliya Whiteley:

Collections
Witchcraft in the Harem (Dog Horn Publishing, 2013)

Novellas
The Arrival of Missives (Unsung Stories, 2016; Titan Books, 2018)
The Beauty (Unsung Stories, 2014; Titan Books, 2019)

Novels
Skein Island (Dog Horn Publishing, 2015; Titan Books, 2019)
The Loosening Skin (Unsung Stories, 2018)

Now available and forthcoming from
Black Shuck Shadows:

blackshuckbooks.co.uk/shadows

Lightning Source UK Ltd.
Milton Keynes UK
UKHW020759210721
387515UK00005B/146